Produced by Kroha Associates, Inc.
Middletown, Connecticut

Printed in the United States of America.

ISBN 1-56326-163-4

The Crabby
Conductor

"All right, everyone, please settle down!" shouted Sebastian the crab.

It was the day of the big Seafest Symphony, and rehearsal was not going well. The sea horses kept missing their entrance, and the angelfish were giving Sebastian a devil of a time. "Don't you realize how important this is?" the tiny crab scolded them. "King Triton will be there for the performance! Everything must be perfect!"

Everyone tried to do exactly as Sebastian asked, but no matter how hard they tried, nothing seemed to be good enough for him. Even Ariel, whose voice was as sweet and clear as a bell, couldn't please the crusty crustacean. "No, no, no, no, no!" Sebastian cried halfway through Ariel's solo. "You held that last note too long!"

"It sounded fine to me," Flounder the fish said.

"No talking during rehearsal!" snapped the crab. "It was good, yes, but it wasn't perfect. And I, Horatio Felonious Ignacious Crustaceous Sebastian, will settle for nothing less than perfection!" He leaned in close to Flounder, so that their noses were touching. "And that goes for you, too."

"All right, let's try it again!" cried Sebastian. He raised his baton high in the air, waited until all eyes were on him, and gave the signal to begin.

But no one did.

"Why aren't you playing?" Sebastian asked.

"We're too tired," whined the sea horses as they put away their trumpets and trombones.

"We're hungry and we need to rest!" groaned the angelfish as they packed up their flutes and piccolos. "It's time to have fun!"

"It's okay, Sebastian," Ariel said as she swam away with the others. "We'll be back in plenty of time."

"But we need more practice!" sputtered Sebastian. "Everything must be just right!"

"You worry too much, Sebastian," replied the Little Mermaid. "All work and no play is no fun at all! You need to relax and have some fun." And with that, Ariel and her friends swam off to play hide-and-seek.

Sebastian tried to relax as Ariel told him. But no matter how hard he tried, he just couldn't.

At first he worried that the performance wouldn't be good enough for the king. Then he worried that no one would return in time for the symphony.

He was so worried that he decided to gather everyone
back together while there was still plenty of time.

"Hi, Sebastian!" Scuttle the sea gull cried out when
he spotted the little crab swimming across the lagoon.
"Come and join us! Scales the dragon just made a
fresh batch of seaberry muffins!" Seaberry muffins
were Sebastian's favorite treat, but he couldn't
stop to enjoy them now.

"I can't," replied the crab. "I have
to find Ariel and the others!"

"There you are!" cried Sebastian when he finally caught up with them. "I've been looking for you all afternoon! We have to hurry! The symphony will be starting soon!"

"Can't we play hide-and-seek a little longer?" Flounder asked.

"No," Sebastian said sternly. "Everything has to be perfect, remember?"

"Oh, all right," the Little Mermaid sighed. "But we were only having a little fun!"

Once everyone was finally in place,
Sebastian began to regret that he hadn't
stopped to have a seaberry muffin. He
was so nervous about the symphony that
he hadn't eaten anything all day and now
he was very hungry. But there wasn't
time for him to think about that
now — the symphony was
about to begin!

Sebastian anxiously paced back
and forth while he waited for King Triton
to take his place in the balcony. When the
king finally arrived, the little crab suddenly
felt a bit dizzy, partly because he was so nervous
and partly because he hadn't eaten all day.

"I know I made all of you work very hard,"
Sebastian whispered to the musicians and singers.
"But you'll see — practice makes perfect, and all your
hard work will pay off."

The curtain slowly went up. With a grand wave of his baton, Sebastian began the symphony.

And it *was* perfect! The trumpets trumpeted to perfection. The music of the flutes floated out and filled the hall with sweet sounds. And, as always, Ariel's voice touched a chord in everyone's heart. But then, something started to happen...

Sebastian was so weak from hunger and nervousness that he began
to feel *very* dizzy. "Are you all right, Sebastian?" Ariel said softly.
    "I don't know," replied Sebastian. "I feel kind of…funny."
    The next thing he knew, he lost his balance and
tumbled headfirst
right into the
orchestra!

Ariel rushed forward to catch her tiny friend, but she knocked over a row of music stands instead and sent sea horses and angelfish flying in every direction.

Meanwhile, poor Sebastian had bounced off not one, not two, but *three* drums before landing in the middle of the octopus's big bass drum.

"The symphony!" he wailed. "It's ruined! My whole *life* is ruined! I wanted everything to be perfect — and instead I've made a perfect mess!"

Sebastian looked so silly that the clams couldn't keep from clacking with laughter, and the jellyfish were all jiggling with glee. But worst of all, King Triton was laughing at him, too!

Sebastian had never been so embarrassed in his life. He wished he could just crawl under a shell somewhere and hide.

"I'm so sorry, Your Majesty," Sebastian cried when King Triton arrived on stage. "I wanted so much to please you, but —"

"You most certainly *did* please me!" interrupted the king. "Why, that's the most wonderful symphony I've been to in years!"

"You liked it?" gasped the crab.

"Liked it? I *loved* it!" replied the king. "It's the finest thing you've ever done! Usually these affairs are stuffy things, but this — this was fun!"

"Of course," said Sebastian, taking a bow. "Why should symphonies always be serious?"

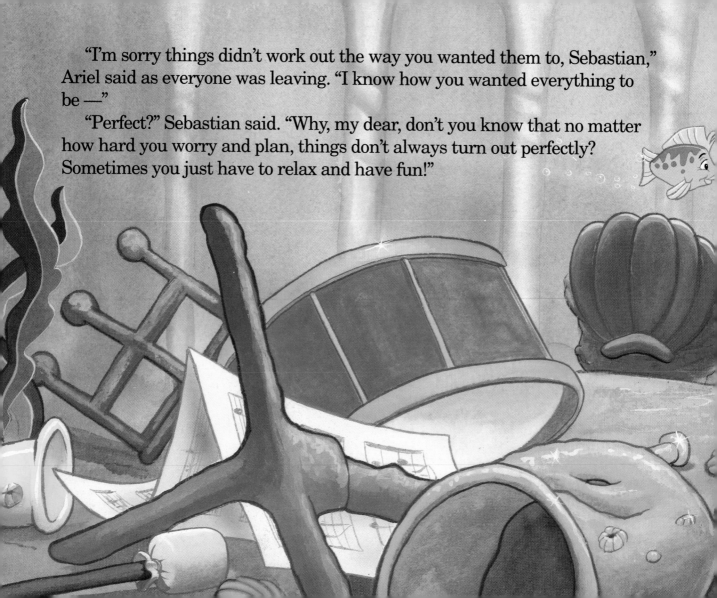

"I'm sorry things didn't work out the way you wanted them to, Sebastian," Ariel said as everyone was leaving. "I know how you wanted everything to be —"

"Perfect?" Sebastian said. "Why, my dear, don't you know that no matter how hard you worry and plan, things don't always turn out perfectly? Sometimes you just have to relax and have fun!"